THE PUPPY PLACE

ANGEL

ELLEN
MILES

SCHOLASTIC INC.

Copyright © 2017 by Ellen Miles
Cover art by Tim O'Brien
Original cover design by Steve Scott

ISBN 978-1-338-06919-8

10 9 8 7 6 5 4 3 2 1   17 18 19 20 21

Printed in the U.S.A.   40
First printing 2017

CHAPTER ONE

Ms. Sharma stopped suddenly in the middle of the path and held up her hand to let everyone else know that they should stop, too. She turned her face to the sky. *"Spshsh!"* She made a funny noise with her mouth. *"Spshsh, spshsh!"*

"What's she doing?" Lizzie Peterson leaned over to whisper into the ear of her friend Maria. "What is that noise?"

Maria put a finger over her lips, reminding Lizzie that they were supposed to be on a silent hike. But then she leaned in close to Lizzie's ear and whispered back, "She's calling that bird. See?" She pointed to the crown of a nearby tree.

"That noise is like one that birds make to let each other know that danger is near. When she does it, the birds come out to see what's happening. Birdwatchers call it 'spishing.' My dad does it, too."

Lizzie squinted. Way up in the highest branches, she saw a tiny blob that might have been a bird. Yes! It was moving. It was a bird. It flitted down to a lower branch, then flitted again, perching at last on a branch right over their heads, so Lizzie could see it clearly. It was brown, with white feathers on its chest. It seemed almost as if the bird was responding to Ms. Sharma's noise.

Lizzie shook her head. It couldn't be. Dogs came when you called — that is, they did if they were properly trained — but not wild birds.

"*Spshsh, spshsh,*" said Ms. Sharma again. Another bird popped out of the leaves, and Lizzie froze in place. So did everyone else in her group.

"Wow," breathed Lizzie. The birds were definitely responding. How cool was that? That moment alone made the whole hike worthwhile. It had not been easy getting up at 6:00 A.M. on a Saturday. Finding her hiking boots had been a challenge, too. And the steep, rocky scramble Ms. Sharma had led them on was "no walk in the park," as Lizzie's dad would say.

Except that it was. At least, it was a walk in the Agnes Dimsdale Nature Preserve, which was kind of like a park. Lizzie was there with the Greenies, a new after-school club. It wasn't only for middle grade kids; there were high school students and even a few adults in the club. Their focus was on saving the environment, and Ms. Sharma was the club adviser.

Ms. Sharma was a sixth-grade science teacher. Even before Lizzie had met her, she knew that

Ms. Sharma was famous for knowing everything about the environment and for being passionate about trying to save it. Ms. Sharma had convinced the school to start composting and growing its own vegetables. She had led a campaign to replace all the plastic forks and knives in the cafeteria with special biodegradable utensils that would melt away into nothing when they were thrown out. And every year she planned a huge fund-raiser for the protection of wild tigers.

Lizzie was totally into the idea of helping the environment, and the Greenies had helped her learn about so many ways she could do that. In the past week Lizzie had made her dad promise to build a bigger compost bin in their backyard, asked him to replace all the old lightbulbs in the house with LEDs, and nagged him and Mom to get refillable water bottles.

Most importantly, Lizzie loved and wanted to

protect animals of all kinds — but especially dogs. Dogs were not in danger of going extinct, like tigers were, but some still needed help. The puppies Lizzie's family fostered were examples. The Petersons took care of puppies who needed somewhere to live, just until they could find each one the perfect home. Lizzie was proud of the work her family did. It was never easy to give up the puppies when it was time, but it always felt good to know that they were going to a safe, loving place.

"Spshsh, spshsh!" Ms. Sharma made the noise again, and three more birds appeared.

Lizzie smiled. Once again, she had been lost in daydreaming about dogs. Her mom always said that Lizzie could not go five minutes without thinking about dogs or puppies. Everything reminded her of dogs — even those little brown birds! Their coloring was so much like Buddy's.

Buddy was an adorable puppy, brown with a white heart-shaped spot on his chest. The Petersons had fostered Buddy, but just that once, they had not given up the puppy: Buddy had become part of the family. Lizzie liked to think he was her dog, but really she shared him with her two younger brothers, Charles and the Bean.

She wished she could have brought Buddy on the hike, but Ms. Sharma had said that dogs were not invited this time. "We will be moving silently through the woods, using all our senses to take in what's around us," she'd explained when Lizzie asked. "A dog might be too much of a distraction. Also, dogs often frighten off wildlife."

Now Lizzie could see that Ms. Sharma had been right. This hike had been different from any hike she'd been on before. Instead of chatting as they walked, they had been completely quiet. She had paid attention to the sound of dirt crunching under her feet, and the feel of a cool breeze on her face. She had noticed the musty smell of dried leaves, and the bright taste of the spruce buds Ms. Sharma had handed around, and the sight of sun sparkling on shiny green leaves.

At a few points they had stopped and gathered in a circle while Ms. Sharma pointed out a certain plant that could be used to cure sore throats, or taught them how to tell the difference between a maple tree and a cherry tree just by looking at the bark. She showed them mushrooms growing, scratches made by a deer rubbing his antlers against a young sapling, and even some coyote poop (or scat, as she called it) right in the middle of the trail. "You can tell this is from a coyote because of all the little hairs in it. See?" She poked at it with a stick. "That's because they eat mice and rabbits, along with berries and fruit and anything else they can find."

"Ewww!" said some of the other kids on the hike. But Lizzie knelt down to take a closer look. She picked up a stick and poked at the scat, just like Ms. Sharma.

"Cool," she said. "I can see apple seeds in there."

They hiked on, climbing higher and higher through the trees until they arrived at a wide-open spot edged by high cliffs. "This is about as far as we'll go today," said Ms. Sharma. "The rest of the trail can be a little rugged for a first hike." She pulled three pairs of binoculars out of her backpack. "Also, it's getting close to nesting time for peregrine falcons, so it's better to stay away for now. They nest up on those steep cliffs, believe it or not. We may even be able to see one if we look carefully." She passed out the binoculars. "Peregrine falcons are beautiful birds, the fastest flyers in the bird world."

Lizzie was lucky enough to be standing right

next to Ms. Sharma, so she got to be first with a pair of binoculars. She put them to her eyes, focused them, and looked up at the cliffs, scanning from right to left in hopes of seeing a falcon. *Could you call falcons by going* spshsh, spshsh? She was just about to ask Ms. Sharma when something caught her eye — a blob of white on a high ledge, almost near the top of the cliff. She looked, then looked again, turning the knob on her binoculars for better focus. Then she drew in a breath.

"Ms. Sharma," she said, "there's a dog on that cliff!"

CHAPTER TWO

"A dog?" Ms. Sharma shook her head. "I don't think so, Lizzie. What would a dog be doing up on that steep cliff?"

Maria was looking through another pair of binoculars. "I think she's right, Ms. Sharma. I think it's a dog!" She handed the binoculars to Ms. Sharma.

The teacher peered through the binoculars. She gasped. "Oh, dear!" she said. "It is a dog — a little white dog. It must be trapped there. Is it moving? Is it — "

"Alive?" Lizzie finished. "Yes! I can see her

shivering. Poor thing. She must be terrified. I wonder how long she's been stuck there."

Ms. Sharma handed the binoculars back to Maria and pulled out her phone. "I'm calling 911," she said. "That dog needs help." She punched in the numbers. "I'm so glad I have a phone signal here. There's no way we could save that dog by ourselves." She glanced up at the cliff again and shook her head. "Hello?" she said into the phone. "I want to report an animal in trouble."

Lizzie kept her binoculars trained on the dog while Ms. Sharma talked to the 911 dispatcher. The closer she looked, the more she was convinced that the dog was just a puppy. Her long coat was white — or at least it would have been if it hadn't been so dirty — and straggly, matted in places. She was small and thin, and she looked so afraid. Lizzie's heart went out to the frightened little dog.

"I think I should call my dad, too," she said when Ms. Sharma finished her call. "He knows all the rescue guys." Lizzie was thinking of the time when her family had been having a winter picnic at a lake near their house. They had spotted a puppy who had fallen through the ice, and her dad, a firefighter, had known just who to call. The cold-water rescue team had saved the puppy, and the Petersons had fostered him. Lizzie had really fallen in love with that puppy, Noodle.

Ms. Sharma handed over her phone. "Go ahead," she said. "I think this puppy needs all the help she can get."

Lizzie dialed. "Dad!" she said when he answered.

"Lizzie!" Dad said. "Are you all right?"

"Yes! No! I mean yes," Lizzie said. "The hike is going great. I'm fine, everybody's fine. Except for this puppy. She's stuck on a cliff, and — "

"Where are you?" Dad suddenly sounded very businesslike, as if he already had his EMT backpack on and one foot out the door.

"Um . . . where are we?" Lizzie looked at Ms. Sharma, and the teacher gestured for the phone. Lizzie handed it over.

"We are on the Embankment Trail at Dimsdale park," Ms. Sharma said. "We're at the base of the cliffs, and the dog seems to be trapped about three-quarters of the way up, toward the eastern end. It'll be much quicker if the rescuers go to the top of the cliffs. You can drive straight into the viewpoint parking area there." She listened for a moment. "Yes, I already called 911. Yes, we'll stay right here. No, I won't let Lizzie try to climb the cliff."

As upset as she was, Lizzie had to smile at that. Her dad knew her so well. He knew she could not stand to see an animal in trouble. If she could have climbed the cliff, she would have, but it was obvious that there was no way up that steep rocky face — not without ropes and special gear. All she could do was stare through the binoculars and murmur, "Hang on, little puppy! We'll help you. Don't worry." Lizzie thought it was a lucky thing that the puppy looked so exhausted. If she was tired, she was less likely to try to move off the tiny ledge she was stuck on. "How did she even get there?" Lizzie asked, almost to herself.

"If there's a parking area up there, she might have jumped out of her people's car. Maybe she was chasing a squirrel or something," said Maria. "She might have not even noticed that the cliff was there until it was too late."

Lizzie looked at her and nodded. "I can totally imagine Buddy doing that," she said. "You know how he is. Whenever he spots a squirrel, it's like the rest of his brain turns off. All he wants to do is chase that squirrel." That was one reason Lizzie always kept Buddy on a leash unless they were in their own fenced yard. She knew he would probably run right across a busy street if he saw a squirrel on the other side.

She swung the binoculars up again and watched the trembling dog. *What if Buddy was trapped on a cliff like that?* Lizzie's heart thudded as she thought about it.

"Look!" Caytlin, one of the other Greenies, pointed to the top of the cliff. "Somebody's here already!"

Lizzie aimed the binoculars at the highest edge of the cliff. Sure enough, several men and women, dressed in red jackets and carrying ropes and other equipment, had appeared. They waved and hooted, and Lizzie and the Greenies waved and hooted back. One of the women lay down on the cliff and inched her way forward until she could see over its lip. She scanned the cliff face with her binoculars.

"To your right!" called Ms. Sharma.

The rescuer looked through her binoculars until she spotted the dog. Then she sat up and motioned to the rest of the team, pointing to the ledge where the puppy was stuck.

Lizzie checked on the puppy through her binoculars. She held her breath, afraid that the puppy would try to move. But the puppy just cowered, shivering, as if she was trying to push herself even closer to the cliff.

"Hey, there!"

Lizzie spun around at her dad's voice. "Daddy!" she said. She ran to him and flung her arms around him. "I'm so glad you're here."

Dad hugged her tight. "Me, too," he said. He was breathing hard after the fast hike uphill. He glanced up at the cliff. "Oh, great, Neal's team is already here. They're the best people for this job. They do all kinds of backcountry rescue, and they really know their stuff."

"How will they save the puppy?" asked James, another Greenie.

"They'll do it all with ropes," dad said. "These folks are all experienced rock climbers and they know how to rig ropes so they can scramble down that cliff safely. The main question is whether the dog will stay still as they get closer."

"I think she will," Lizzie said. "She's really scared and she doesn't seem to want to move at all." She handed the binoculars to her dad, and he took a look.

He nodded. "That's good. If she doesn't try to squirm away from the rescuers, they'll have an easier time getting a harness on her. Once that's done, she'll be safely roped in, too, and they can decide whether to pull her up to the top or lower her down to us."

Lizzie knew which one she was hoping for. She couldn't wait to hold that terrified little puppy in her arms. She turned her face up to see how the dog was doing and noticed a splash of red against the rock face. "Look!" she said. "Somebody's starting down the cliff!"

CHAPTER THREE

Lizzie reached for the binoculars, but her dad was already focusing them on the red blob on the cliff. "That looks like Rose," he said. "She's a terrific climber, and she's also great with animals. Perfect choice."

"Let me see, let me see," Lizzie begged. Dad handed her the binoculars and she put them to her eyes, scanning the cliff face for a better look at Rose. There she was! She wore a harness that was clipped into a rope. Her teammates held the rope from above, slowly letting it out as Rose inched her way down the wall of rock, grabbing at any cracks or bulges and using each handhold to help steer her way.

Lizzie held her breath as she watched. Rose sure was brave. Lizzie wasn't sure she could ever do that, even if she was securely hitched into a harness and supported by strong ropes. What if you looked down? Wouldn't you get dizzy? The cliffs were so high and steep.

Lizzie kept moving the binoculars back and forth between Rose and the puppy. She noticed that the puppy seemed too exhausted to pay attention to the person who was getting nearer and nearer. Lizzie could see a pink tongue hanging out and noticed that the puppy's chest was moving; that meant the puppy was panting. She was probably thirsty, but Lizzie knew that panting was also a sign of stress. "Hang tight, little girl," she murmured as she watched. "Just stay still, and you'll be safe and sound any minute now."

She switched back to watch Rose again. Boy, was she strong. She climbed down the cliff face like a spider, her wiry body clinging to the rocks as she moved along. She stepped out one long leg, searching for a foothold. Then her arm shot out to find a spot where her hand could grab. It was almost like a dance. Lizzie could see the determination on Rose's face whenever she craned her neck to check on the dog. She saw Rose's lips move, and even though she couldn't hear what the woman was saying, she was sure she knew. Rose was saying the same things Lizzie was: "Stay still, little puppy. You'll be safe soon."

When Lizzie switched back to see how the puppy was doing, she hardly had to move the binoculars at all. Rose was getting close!

"What will Rose do when she gets there?" Lizzie asked her dad.

"See the orange rope hanging from her belt?"

Dad said. "When she reaches the puppy, she'll make a harness out of that and loop it around the dog's body. When it's secure, she'll clip it into her rope. That's the trickiest part. If the puppy struggles or tries to get away . . ."

He didn't say any more. He didn't have to. Lizzie gulped, imagining that tiny white body falling, falling, falling. No! It wasn't going to happen. She was sure that Rose would be able to get the harness on. She held her breath as Rose inched closer to the dog. Now she could see them both without moving the binoculars at all. Rose had reached the spot where the dog cowered on the tiny ledge. She braced her feet against the cliff face just below the puppy.

"She made it!" said Dad. "See how she's tugging on the rope to let the others know she's there?"

Lizzie nodded, but she couldn't speak. Her heart pounded as she watched Rose. She took another deep breath. "Here we go, puppy," she whispered. "Rose is going to help you. Just don't move, whatever you do!"

Slowly, Rose reached out a hand to let the dog sniff her. Lizzie could see Rose's lips moving again, and she knew that Rose was murmuring comforting words to the frightened puppy.

The puppy trembled harder than ever but didn't try to pull away from Rose. She seemed to be frozen in place, too frightened to move.

Rose petted the puppy for a few moments, then unclipped the coil of orange rope from her belt. She looped it around the puppy's chest, working swiftly but gently. With a few quick expert knots, she had created a strong harness.

"Now she'll clip the puppy to her own ropes, using that metal loop," said Dad. "That's called a carabiner, and it will guarantee that the puppy stays with her."

A moment later, Rose was again tugging on the rope.

"That's to tell them that she's all set," said Dad. He squeezed Lizzie's shoulder. "She did it! The puppy is going to be fine."

Lizzie let out her breath in a big whoosh, but she knew she would not be able to really relax until that dog was in her arms. "Are they going to lower her down or pull her up?" she asked Dad.

"It looks like they're getting ready to help her climb down safely." Dad pointed to some red-coated people who had arrived at the base of the cliff. They caught the end of a very long rope that the top people had tossed down. Lizzie looked back up at Rose and saw that she was clipped into that rope now. "They'll be able to help control Rose's speed and stop her from falling if she slips."

By then Rose had tucked the puppy, harness and all, inside her jacket. The little white head stuck out as the puppy peered around. Lizzie could just imagine how secure she must feel against the warmth of Rose's chest. What a difference from the hard, cold rocks!

Rose was dancing again, stepping down the cliff with grace and confidence as the people below held her ropes taut. Now her descent was much quicker. In moments, she had landed on the ground. Her teammates surrounded her, slapping her on the back and cheering, as she stepped out of her climbing harness.

The Greenies cheered, too. Lizzie felt tears rolling down her face. The puppy was safe. The puppy was safe!

Lizzie handed her binoculars to Maria. "Let's go," she said to Dad. "That puppy needs us."

CHAPTER FOUR

"Great work," Dad said to Rose when he and Lizzie reached her.

Lizzie held out her arms. "Can I hold the puppy?" she asked.

"Lizzie!" Dad shook his head, smiling. "This is my daughter, Lizzie," he said to Rose. "She's a little dog-crazy."

Rose smiled. "I understand. So am I. And who wouldn't want to hold this little pup? She's adorable, even though she's all matted and dirty." Rose sat down on the ground, pulled the puppy out of her jacket, and gently undid the knots holding the harness together. "There you go, little one," she said. "She's going to need some extra care over the next few days. I'm sure she's starving, and — "

"Dehydrated," said Lizzie. "She needs water right away." Lizzie sat down, too, and pulled a water bottle out of her backpack. "Can you pour some into my hands?" she asked Rose. "Maybe we can get her to drink."

The puppy stood on wobbly legs, gazing uncertainly around. She took a few steps toward Lizzie, then plopped down on her butt.

Whoo! My legs aren't working so well.

Lizzie and Rose laughed. "It's like she almost forgot how to walk because of sitting on that ledge for so long, but she'll remember soon enough," said Rose. She poured some water into Lizzie's cupped hands.

Lizzie held out her hands to the puppy. "Drink up, cutie," she said.

The puppy looked up at Lizzie and cocked her head. She was absolutely adorable, with her floppy ears and black nose and round shiny black eyes. She bowed her head to Lizzie's hands, and her little pink tongue shot out to taste the water. She lapped eagerly until Lizzie's hands were empty. Rose poured out more water, and the puppy lapped that up, too. Lizzie felt her heart melting as she watched the scraggly little pup. She was so trusting and sweet!

After she had drunk her fill, the puppy stood up again and took a few more steps, as if checking to see whether her legs were working better. "Hey, puppy!" called Maria, who was standing nearby. The puppy turned to look up at Maria, then ran right toward her, bouncing along as if she did not have a care in the world.

Whee! I'm on the ground again. What a great place to be! What a beautiful day!

Everybody laughed and applauded when they saw the puppy running. All the Greenies, Ms. Sharma, Lizzie's dad, and the other rescuers crowded around to watch. She trotted from person to person, greeting each one with a wagging tail and a shake of her head.

"Look at her go!" said James.

"She's so happy to be off that cliff!" said Ms. Sharma.

"Such a cutie," said Maria as she caught the puppy up in her arms and snuggled her face into her fur.

"Did you see the way she runs?" Rose asked Lizzie. "I was thinking that she might be a Havanese, and now I'm almost positive."

Lizzie grinned. Rose really was dog-crazy. Just

like Lizzie, she knew her dog breeds. "I bet you're right," she said. "I remember reading that Havanese have that bouncy gait because their front legs are a little longer than the back ones." Lizzie had never met a Havanese before, but she'd always wanted to. According to her "Dog Breeds of the World" poster, it was the national dog of Cuba and known as an affectionate little clown.

"Does she have a collar?" asked Dad. "I wonder what her name is and where she came from."

Maria checked. "No collar," she said.

Just then, a tall woman in a brown uniform hiked into the clearing and approached the group. "Well, well," she said. "I just got news of this over my radio. I'm Julie, the ranger here." She knelt down to pet the puppy. "What an exciting morning you've had," she said to the dog. She looked up at Rose, who was coiling up her ropes. "Did you bring her down? Nice job," Julie said, when Rose nodded.

"Does this dog belong to anyone you know?" Dad asked.

Julie shook her head. "She's a stray, I think," she said. "We've had people tell us they've seen her here and there in the park for the last two weeks, but we haven't been able to catch her. We were hoping that somebody who camped here might have lost her and might come looking for her, but nobody has turned up. I hate to say it, but maybe she was dumped here. It wouldn't be the first time that happened."

"You mean people just leave dogs in the park?" Maria asked. "That's terrible! If they don't want the dog anymore, why don't they take her to an animal shelter so somebody else can adopt her?"

Julie shrugged. "Some people just aren't thinking, I guess. It's a real shame."

"Well, the first thing we'll need to do is get her checked for a microchip," Lizzie said, "just in case she wasn't dumped. Maybe somebody is looking for her. We should stop at Dr. Gibson's office first so the vet can give her a whole checkup. Then on the way home we can pick up some small-breed puppy food. And maybe some new toys. Buddy shouldn't always have to share his toys with our foster puppies."

"Our — what?" Dad asked. "Lizzie, we haven't even discussed this with each other yet, much less with the rest of the family. I'm getting the picture, though. I think you would like us to foster this puppy."

"Of course!" said Lizzie. She took the puppy from Maria's arms. "Where else is she going to go? And I've already figured out her name. We'll call her Angel, because she must have a very special guardian angel of her own."

Rose walked over to pet Angel one more time. "When you're ready to find a new home for Angel, let me know," she said. "I might just have an idea about that."

"Really? Do you want to adopt her right now?" Lizzie asked.

Rose shook her head. "I wish I could, but I can't," she said. "I've got a big training weekend coming up, and for the moment I'm working two other jobs. But please keep me posted on what happens with her."

"After what you did to rescue her, you definitely deserve first dibs on this puppy," said Lizzie. "I promise we won't give her away without checking with you."

CHAPTER FIVE

The hike down the hill was a lot faster than the hike up. Lizzie and her dad led the way, followed by the rest of the Greenies and the team that had rescued Angel. Lizzie carried the little pup the whole way, cradling her in her arms. "You're going to be fine," she whispered to Angel. "We'll take good care of you, and if you have owners, we'll find them, and if you don't, we'll find you the perfect home. You don't have to worry about a thing."

Angel did not seem worried. She snuggled into Lizzie's arms and enjoyed the ride, stretching up her neck now and then to give Lizzie a kiss on the cheek.

Thanks for the lift, friend!

Lizzie giggled every time she did that, since Angel's silky fur tickled her face. "You are a total lovebug, aren't you?" asked Lizzie. She knew that Havanese had been bred as lapdogs and companion animals, so that made sense. Still, she had never met a dog who was quite so happy to snuggle.

When they reached Dad's pickup, parked near Ms. Sharma's van, Dad smiled down at Lizzie. "Well, it looks like you two have already bonded," he said. "I guess that means we really do have a new foster puppy. I'm sure Mom will agree as soon as she sees this cutie."

"Yay!" Lizzie grinned at Maria. "Want to come over and play with her?" she asked. "We could give her a bath. She really needs one."

"Maybe later on," said Maria. "I have a riding lesson this afternoon."

"And weren't we going to stop at the vet and the pet store?" Dad reminded Lizzie. He opened the door of the truck for her.

Lizzie was about to get in when another van pulled into the parking lot, a big white one with a satellite dish mounted on top. A man and a woman jumped out and slammed the doors. "Where's the miracle puppy?" the woman asked. She held up a video camera. "We're from WCBT TV. Can we get an interview with the rescuers?"

Dad looked surprised. "Wow, news travels fast," he said.

Julie, the ranger, stepped forward. "I called them," she explained. "As soon as I heard about the dog trapped on the cliff, I knew it would make a great story." She turned to the man, who held a microphone. "I'm Julie. I was hoping you'd get here in time to film the rescue."

He stuck out his hand for a shake. "Richie Whitcomb. We came as fast as we could," he said. "No problemo. If we can do a couple of interviews, I can find some visuals to go along with them. We'll hike up and film the cliffs. Maybe some of you guys can come along." He gestured to the rescue team. "Which one of you fellas is the hero?" he asked.

The guys on the team pushed Rose forward.

"A gal! Even better." He held up the microphone, and the woman with the camera stepped closer to Rose. "Tell us all about it. Were you scared on that big steep cliff?"

Rose rolled her eyes. "First of all, I'm not a 'gal.' I'm a woman, and I'm the best climber on our team. And, no, I wasn't afraid. The only thing that worried me was whether the dog would stay still enough for me to get a harness on her."

The man nodded. "Good, good. Tell me more about it. Wait — where's the dog? Let's get the dog in the shot." He looked around and spotted Lizzie, who was still holding Angel. He waved her over. "Right there, little girl," he said. "Stand next to that, uh, woman."

It was Lizzie's turn to roll her eyes. She did not like being called a little girl. She stayed right where she was. "I'm not a little girl," she said. "I'm Lizzie. Lizzie Peterson. I have a dog-walking business and my family fosters puppies. This is Angel. We think she's a stray, and my family is going to be taking care of her."

"Oh, we have a name for the pooch? Great, great. Perfect. Love it. Did you get that, Edie?"

"Got it." The woman with the camera nodded. "Lizzie, if you'd be willing to just stand right next to Rose, I can get a nice shot of you and the dog."

Lizzie liked the way Edie spoke to her. "Sure," she said. She went to stand by Rose. They grinned at each other. "I guess Angel is going to be famous," said Lizzie.

"I guess we all are, whether we like it or not," said Rose.

"Here we go!" said Richie. Rose and Lizzie turned to face him. "Keep smiling," he directed.

Lizzie smiled. It was easy to smile when she had an adorable puppy in her arms. She cuddled Angel closer, and the puppy stretched up to lick her cheek. Rose leaned over to give Angel a kiss, and Angel licked her cheek, too. That made them both smile even harder.

"Great, great," said the man. "Terrific. What a

shot! I love it. Grateful dog, happy rescuer, and the little — I mean, the person who's going to care for the pup." He held the microphone to Lizzie's face. "So tell me, how did the whole rescue happen? I mean, how did you even know that there was a dog on the cliff?"

"I saw her!" said Lizzie. "I spotted her with binoculars."

"And what were you doing all the way out here in the middle of nowhere?" asked Richie.

"I was on a hike with my club the Greenies," Lizzie said. "We're an ecology club. We want to help save the environment, and — "

"Good, fine," said Richie. "And then what happened, after you saw the dog?"

Lizzie didn't like the way he interrupted her, but she answered his next question anyway. "We called the rescuers," said Lizzie. "I couldn't believe how fast they got here."

Richie switched to Rose. "And then you whipped into action," he said, "like some kind of spider woman. Amazing! Tell our viewers how you did it."

Rose began to explain how the roping setup worked, and how every team member was an important part of the rescue. Richie nodded. "But you were the one who climbed down the cliff," he said. "Come on, you're a heroine. Don't be shy! Tell us all about it."

He held up the microphone while Rose talked him through the rescue. Then he went back to Lizzie. "And now the little pooch will be going home with you," he said.

"Just temporarily," said Lizzie. "We are a foster family, and we may be looking for a home for her — that is, if we can't find her owners."

"Well, that shouldn't be hard," said Richie. "This little doggy is going to be a big hit on the news tonight, you can be sure of that. People will be knocking down your door to get to her." He gave the camerawoman the "cut" sign.

"Don't forget I have first dibs!" Rose said. She leaned over to give Angel another smooch.

"You bet," Dad told Rose. He put his arm around Lizzie's shoulders. "I think the interview is over," he told Richie. "We need to get both of these girls home."

CHAPTER SIX

"Oh, no, she's leaving!" Lizzie's heart sank. Her dad had just pulled up to Dr. Gibson's office, but the vet was on her way out, locking the front door.

Dad slapped his forehead. "Of course! It's Saturday. She's only open until one."

Lizzie unclipped her seat belt and jumped out of the pickup as soon as Dad parked. "Dr. Gibson!" she called as she ran up the walk with Angel in her arms. The little white pup had spent the ride dozing contentedly after her long ordeal. Lizzie knew she must be exhausted from all the excitement and from her time on the ledge. How long had she been there? Lizzie could hardly stand the thought of that sweet, loving pup alone on a cold rocky ledge all through the night — or through several nights and days!

Dr. Gibson turned around, spotted Lizzie, and smiled. Then she saw Angel, and her smile widened. "Well, well, well, what do we have here?" she asked. She put down her briefcase and tote bag and walked down the porch steps to greet them.

"Her name's Angel," Lizzie said. "I think she's a Havanese. She was trapped on a ledge on some really, really steep cliffs, and — "

"Is she okay?" Dr. Gibson reached out for the dog, and Lizzie handed her over. "Did she fall? Is she hurt?" The vet was checking Angel all over, touching her head, her legs, her tummy.

"No, she was rescued," said Lizzie. "Dad's friend Rose climbed down the cliff and put a harness on her and lowered her down. It was so awesome. I wish you could have seen it." Lizzie's words were tumbling over each other in her excitement, but Dr. Gibson just nodded.

"I wonder how long she was up there," she said, almost to herself, as she shifted Angel to her other arm, reached into her pocket for a key, and unlocked the door. "She feels a little underweight, and I'm sure she's probably — "

"Dehydrated! That's what I thought," said Lizzie. "She really perked up when we gave her some water but I'm sure she needs more."

"Maybe we should keep her overnight, get her on some IV fluids," Dr. Gibson said as Lizzie and her dad followed her into one of the clinic's exam rooms.

"No!" The word burst out of Lizzie. She was already crazy about the little pup and couldn't stand the thought of her spending the night in the clinic with tubes running into her. "I mean, I'd really like to take her home. I'll do anything you tell me, and I promise to take care of her."

Dr. Gibson grinned at Lizzie. "I should have figured. Well, I'll give her some fluids right now while I examine her, and then if everything looks all right, I'll send her home with you."

"Speaking of which, weren't you on your way home?" Dad asked.

Dr. Gibson shrugged. "I always have time for a puppy," she said. "Especially a Peterson puppy." She let Lizzie hold Angel in her arms as she hooked up the puppy to an IV line, putting in the needle so expertly that Angel didn't even seem to notice. Fluids began to drip from a clear plastic bag, through tubing, right into Angel's leg. "Okay, that's set," said Dr. Gibson. She went back to checking Angel. "Aren't you sweet?" she murmured as she knelt down to listen to Angel's lungs with a stethoscope. She also looked into her ears and eyes and checked her tummy.

Angel took it all in stride, sitting calmly on

Lizzie's lap while Dr. Gibson looked her over. She even wagged her tail when Dr. Gibson was inspecting her teeth, then kissed Dr. Gibson on the cheek as if to thank her for the checkup.

I love attention — any kind!

"She seems fine," said Dr. Gibson. "She's a real trouper, this one. Not many puppies her age could go through what she went through and still be so sweet and loving." The vet frowned. "It's hard to believe someone would abandon such a great pup, and a purebred at that. I think you were right about her being a Havanese. Once you give her a bath, you'll see how silky her coat will be."

"Can we check her for a microchip?" Lizzie's dad asked.

"Sure," said Dr. Gibson. She reached into a drawer for the wand she used to check for the tiny chip that would tell her how to find a lost dog's owners. If Angel had caring owners, they might have had a chip implanted. Dr. Gibson bent over to wave the wand over Angel's head and body, then waved it again, more slowly. She shook her head. "No chip, and I didn't see a tattoo on her, either. No way to know if she has a family."

She straightened up and opened the laptop on her counter. "I always check Facebook for missing dog alerts," she said. "I haven't seen any recently, but let's look again. We can post her picture, too, with a description of where she was found. It's amazing how quickly word can spread through the Internet."

"She's going to be on the news, too," Lizzie told the vet. She explained about the TV crew.

"Excellent," said Dr. Gibson. "If she has owners, they're sure to step forward to claim her. And if not, you'll have no trouble finding her a new home. Such a sweetie!" She used her phone to snap a few pictures of Angel in Lizzie's arms, then showed them to Lizzie and her dad. "She looks great in pictures, too — even before a bath!"

Lizzie helped pick the best picture, and Dr. Gibson posted it on the missing dogs page with a little background on where she had been found and how she had been rescued. "If anyone's looking for her, we've done what we can," Dr. Gibson said when she was finished. "I'll notify the police and animal control, and I'm sure you'll be checking in with Ms. Dobbins."

Ms. Dobbins was the director of Caring Paws, the animal shelter where Lizzie volunteered. Lizzie put her hand over her mouth. "Oh, no! I was supposed to help out there today after our hike! With all the excitement I totally forgot."

"We can call Ms. Dobbins as soon as we leave here," Dad said.

"If anyone would understand, she would," said Dr. Gibson. "Animals always come first in her book."

"Mine, too," said Lizzie, looking down at the sweet white puppy nestled in her lap. What was more important than taking care of an animal who needed help?

CHAPTER SEVEN

Lizzie and Dad stopped by Caring Paws after their visit to the pet store. "Of course I understand," said Ms. Dobbins when Lizzie apologized again for missing her volunteer shift. "What an exciting day you've had, all of you." She gave Angel a scratch between the ears. "And you've lucked out," she told the white puppy. "You're going home to the best foster family ever." She smiled at Lizzie. "I doubt you'll have any trouble finding this cutie a home," she said, "but let me know if I can help."

Lizzie thanked her. "There's one thing you can

do," she said, "but it's not to do with Angel. It's those." She pointed to a roll of paper towels on the counter at the shelter's front desk. "They're not very environmentally friendly. Could you switch to using rags? They can be washed instead of thrown away."

Ms. Dobbins looked surprised. "Well . . . I don't know," she said. "You know we have a lot of messes to clean up around here. But I guess we could try."

"Great," said Lizzie. "Also, maybe you could think about switching to white vinegar for cleaning up those messes. Some of those cleaning sprays are full of terrible chemicals."

Ms. Dobbins nodded, eyebrows raised.

Lizzie kept talking. "See, in my new club, the Greenies, we have a mission to get people to change their habits. We talked about it at our meeting the other day. If each of us can make some small changes, it can make a big difference."

"Okay, Lizzie," said Dad. "I think Ms. Dobbins gets the picture. Ready to head home?" He didn't exactly roll his eyes, but Lizzie knew he was already a little tired of hearing about environmental living.

Lizzie nodded. "But you should come to the Greenies booth at the Wellness Fair next week," she told Ms. Dobbins. "We'll have a bunch of handouts about all the ways you can make your house and workplace more environmentally friendly."

Dad pulled on Lizzie's sleeve. "Let's go," he said. He waved good-bye to Ms. Dobbins.

Maria showed up soon after Dad and Lizzie got home. By then, the entire Peterson family was already in love with Angel. She had the perfect personality! She dashed around the yard with Buddy, and they played together as if they'd been besties forever. She was gentle with the Bean and, once they had gotten to know each other, even let him play with her tail. Charles loved the way she jumped into his lap the minute he sat down, and Mom (who was usually more of a cat person) was already saying that Angel was the sweetest, cutest puppy they had ever fostered.

"And she still hasn't even had her bath!" Lizzie told Maria. "She's going to be cuteness overload when she's all cleaned and groomed."

Lizzie and Maria played with Angel and Buddy in the backyard for a while, trying to tire out the puppy so she would be calm during her bath. The new friends wrestled and ran, chasing each other back and forth. "I love the way she runs!"

Maria said. "It's like she has springs in her feet. She's so bouncy."

"And her ears flop in the cutest way," Lizzie said. "She looks like a cartoon dog."

Angel seemed to know they were talking about her. She trotted over with a big puppy grin on her face. Then she did a play bow to Lizzie, stretching out her front paws and sticking her butt in the air.

Aren't you going to throw that for me? I love fetching!

Lizzie looked down at the ball in her hand and laughed. "I guess she wants to chase this," she said. She tossed it to Angel, and the little dog pranced after it. The ball was almost as big as her head, but she grabbed it in her teeth and carried it back, bouncing along with her tail arched proudly.

See? I'm good at this, right?

She brought the ball to Lizzie, then climbed into Maria's lap, stretching up for a kiss.

Enough of this running around. I'm ready to cuddle.

Then it was Maria's turn to laugh. "I just sat down a second ago!" she said.

"I know," said Lizzie. "As soon as Angel sees a lap, she wants to lie down on it."

Maria petted Angel. "What a cuddle-bug." She scratched between the puppy's ears. "Have you thought of any fun ideas for the Greenies booth?" she asked. "I'm going to make a poster about how many tons of garbage could be kept out of the landfills if people recycled even one percent more."

Lizzie nodded. "Cool," she said. "I have an idea, too — but it's secret for now." She did not actually have an idea, but she didn't want Maria to know that. Lizzie was an idea person; she knew she would come up with something great. Sometimes it just took a while.

"Bath time, Angel," Lizzie called. She patted her knees, and Angel jumped off Maria's lap and leapt into hers. Both girls cracked up.

Angel was a good puppy at bath time. She stayed calm as Lizzie and Maria stood her in the half-full tub and soaked her with water they poured from rinsed-out yogurt containers. "I finally got my mom to buy the larger size of yogurt," Lizzie told Maria as they poured. "So we only have one container to recycle instead of six."

"That's great," said Maria. "And I convinced my parents to start hanging the laundry out on a clothesline instead of using the dryer."

Angel stood shivering in the tub. She looked much skinnier with her coat wet. She gazed up at Lizzie, cocked her head, and wagged her tail.

Can we please get on with the bath?

Maria squeezed a dab of the Bean's baby shampoo onto Angel's coat and began to massage it in. They soaped her up well, then rinsed her, again pouring the warm water over her fur.

"Wow, look at the water turning black," said Lizzie. "I guess she really was dirty. Maybe we'd better soap her up again."

By the second rinse, Angel had lost patience. She began to squirm out of their hands, clawing at the tub as she tried to get out. "Okay, okay," said Lizzie as she helped the wet puppy out of the tub. Lizzie's shirt was soaked by the time she had set Angel on the bath mat.

Angel looked at Lizzie with a twinkle in her shiny black eyes. Then she shook off enthusiastically, spraying water all over Maria.

Ahh, that feels so good!

"Hey!" said Maria, but she was smiling. She wrapped Angel in a big fluffy blue towel and dried her off. When Maria was done, Angel shook herself again.

"Aww, look at her!" said Lizzie. "She's gorgeous!" Angel's silky coat glowed bright white, and her little nose and button eyes looked blacker and shinier than ever.

"Meanwhile, check us out!" Maria said. She and Lizzie faced the bathroom mirror and cracked up again. They both had big wet splotches all over their shirts. Maria's hair was wildly tangled, and one of Lizzie's braids had come undone.

"Lizzie," Mom called up the stairs just then. "We need you downstairs. Guess who's here? It's Richie Whitcomb. He wants to interview you again. Right now! Live!"

Lizzie and Maria stared at each other. Then they burst out laughing. "Well, at least Angel looks good," said Maria.

CHAPTER EIGHT

"Hurry!" Mom called.

Lizzie was still in the bathroom, frantically try-ing to re-braid her hair. The faster she tried to braid, the more tangled her hair became. "Oh, forget it," she said to Maria. "You were right. The only thing that matters is that Angel looks good. This story is all about her."

She grabbed her hairbrush and gave her hair a few strokes. She frowned down at her wet shirt, then shrugged. "Oh, well," she said, smiling. She picked up Angel and ran down the stairs.

"Just in time," said Richie Whitcomb when Lizzie walked into the living room. The TV was

61

on, and her whole family was crowded on the couch. "The segment is about to air on the news, and then they're going to switch to me for some live reporting. We want to know how Angel is doing after her traumatic experience on the cliff."

He had a different assistant with him this time, a girl with bright blue hair and a big smile. "Hi," she said. "I'm Nina. Cute pup. Take a seat right over here, okay?" She patted the big chair that Lizzie's dad usually sat in.

Lizzie smiled back at her. She liked that blue hair. Maybe Angel would look good with blue hair. Or pink. Maybe pink would be better.

"Here we go," said Richie, pointing at the TV. "As soon as this ad ends. Ready? And three, two, one — "

"A frightening time for a stranded pup," announced the man sitting at the news desk, "and a heroic rescue. It all happened today, at the

Agnes Dimsdale Nature Preserve. Richie Whitcomb was there."

Then there was a film clip of Richie interviewing Rose. She looked confident and strong. "Yay, Rose!" Lizzie whispered. Then she saw herself — on TV! She put her hand over her mouth. That was too weird. "I was on a hike with my club the Greenies," she heard herself say. The rest of the interview went by in a blur, and after some shots of the high cliffs and of Angel, snug in Lizzie's arms, it was over.

"Standing by with the foster family is Richie Whitcomb," the announcer said.

"Here we go," said Nina. She patted Lizzie's head. "You'll do great. Don't worry, and don't think too much. Just answer the questions."

Lizzie took a deep breath and held Angel close.

"Here we are in the Peterson home," said Richie. "This family is well known in the Littleton area for their work with puppies who need help. And here's Lizzie, with the family's latest foster pup."

The camera swung toward Lizzie. She bit her lip. Was she supposed to say something?

Richie spoke again before she had to worry for long. "How is Angel doing now?" he asked. "She had quite an experience today."

"She sure did," said Lizzie. "But she's doing great. She's just a happy little girl, and she loves to cuddle." Lizzie was surprised by how easily the words came out. Being on live TV was no big deal! "We gave her a bath, and she looks terrific." Lizzie held Angel up, smoothing back the adorable cowlick on top of her head. Angel wagged her tail and licked Lizzie's cheek.

Smile! This is our moment!

"Fantastic," said Richie. "And you'll be looking for a home for this little cutie?"

"That's right," said Lizzie. Then she had a fantastic idea. The words popped out before she even thought about it. "And if anyone wants to meet her, we'll be at the Greenies booth at the Wellness Fair on Thursday night. Our environmental club welcomes new members of any age."

Richie raised his eyebrows and nodded. "Very good. I can see you have a natural talent for publicity," he said, smiling. "Angel is lucky to have you in her corner. That's all for now. I'm Richie Whitcomb, reporting live from Littleton." He signaled to the camerawoman that the shoot was over, then moved to shake Lizzie's hand. "Well done," he said.

Lizzie liked him better this time around. At least he wasn't treating her like a kid. "You did a great job, too," she said.

He laughed. "Good luck with finding her a home," he said.

The phone began to ring as soon as Nina and Richie had left, and the very first call was from Rose. "Great work," she said when Lizzie answered. "I'm just calling to remind you that I have first dibs on that dog."

Lizzie gulped. "Um, sure," she said. "Of course." What else could she say? Rose had rescued Angel, after all. But the more Lizzie got to know Angel, the more she worried that Rose might not be the best owner for her. Rose seemed like a person who was always on the go. She worked two jobs on top of being on a rescue crew. That meant her lap would not be available anytime Angel wanted to cuddle.

Would Angel really enjoy being with such an active person? And how would Lizzie ever be able to tell Rose that she might not be the right owner for the dog she had rescued?

That night, as she settled down to sleep with Angel at the foot of her bed, Lizzie tried to forget her worries by replaying the events of the day in her mind. It sure had been an exciting one, maybe the most exciting day of her life. From the moment she'd spotted Angel on that cliff, Lizzie had been swept into adventure after adventure — including a live interview on TV! Who cared if her shirt was wet and her hair was wild? She knew she had rocked that interview. Maybe she had a future in TV news. Lizzie pictured herself in the role of Nina, the blue-haired assistant, eventually working her way up to being a newscaster, like Richie.

That was when Lizzie sat straight up in bed. "Yes!" she said. She had just had one of her best ideas ever, the perfect idea for the Greenies booth.

Angel was so worn out from her exciting day that she barely stirred. She lay curled up, a sweet fluffy white ball of fur. The puppy flicked one floppy ear and blinked one shiny black eye.

Whatever is so exciting, it can wait for tomorrow, right?

Then she curled up even tighter and went to sleep. So did Lizzie — with a big smile on her face.

CHAPTER NINE

"Lizzie, you're going to be late!" Mom called from downstairs.

Once again, Lizzie was in the bathroom, fixing her hair. But this time she was not about to be on live TV. This time she was on her way to the Wellness Fair. She and Maria were supposed to be helping run the Greenies booth, and Mom was right: Lizzie was about to be late. She had finished getting ready just in time, and she was very happy with the results. She grinned at herself in the mirror, holding Angel up so the little dog could see, too. "Of course, you don't know the difference, since dogs are color-blind," said Lizzie, smiling down at the happy pup.

Lizzie's hair, instead of its usual dirty blond, was bright neon green. She turned this way and that, admiring the way her work had turned out. She couldn't wait to see what the other Greenies thought. On the other hand, she was not looking forward to hearing what her mom thought. Even though the hair chalk was temporary and would supposedly wash out easily, Lizzie knew that her mom might be just a tiny bit upset with her for doing it without permission. She bunched her hair into a tight ponytail bun, pulled a baseball cap over it, and smiled at herself again. What a great way to advertise the Greenies!

"We don't really need to advertise you anymore, do we?" Lizzie asked Angel. The phone calls had been pouring in ever since Angel had appeared on TV. Not one call was from a family who had lost Angel, though. Finally, the Petersons had stopped answering the phone and just let voice mail pick up. Lizzie had changed the message to say that Angel was probably spoken for, but that people could leave their information if they were interested in her or in other puppies the Petersons might foster in the future. It never hurt to have a waiting list for puppies who needed homes!

Rose left two messages during the week, promising to come by and see Angel as soon as she could. Her messages were long and confusing, with lots of excuses about why she hadn't come yet and mentions of wanting to talk "in person," but so far she had not shown up at the Petersons'. That made Lizzie worry even more about whether Rose was the perfect owner for Angel. Wasn't she really just too busy to have a dog?

Lizzie had been pretty busy herself, between her dog-walking business, planning for the

Greenies booth at the Wellness Fair, and being with Angel. Angel wasn't a problem puppy like some that the Petersons had fostered; all she wanted was to be near a person, to sit on a lap, or to make somebody laugh by bouncing around in the cutest way possible. She loved attention, and she made Lizzie laugh all the time with her funny ways. "You're a silly girl, aren't you?" Lizzie said to the puppy now, as she hugged Angel closer. "I should have made your hair green to match," she said, rubbing her nose against Angel's silky fur. Angel snuggled into Lizzie's arms.

Um, I don't think so. But thanks anyway.

"Oh, I know. Mom really would have killed me if I'd done that," Lizzie said. She headed for the stairs and slipped out the front door before Mom could spot her. "See you later!" she called as she closed the door behind her.

The Wellness Fair was in Lizzie's school gym, and the place was already packed by the time Lizzie walked in with Angel in her arms and a big bag slung over one shoulder.

There were people giving chair massages, selling vitamins, and handing out brochures for yoga classes. There was a booth where you could make yourself a raspberry-coconut smoothie by pedaling a bike-powered blender. Lizzie saw a few booths she wanted to go back to, including one selling natural flea-control products and one that was giving away free samples of vegan chocolate-chip cookies.

"Wow," said Lizzie to Maria when she'd found her way to the Greenies booth. "There's a lot going on here." She gave Angel to Maria to hold while she pulled off her baseball cap and shook out her hair.

"Wow is right," said Maria, staring at Lizzie's hair.

For a second Lizzie wondered whether she'd made a terrible mistake. Did her hair look ridiculous?

"I love it!" said Maria. "You look amazing."

Lizzie grinned. "And check this out," she said. She emptied out the big bag she'd been carrying. It was full of green hair chalk kits. Lizzie had made a go green label for each one. "We can sell these, or give them away free to people who sign up to be in the club."

"Great idea!" said Ms. Sharma, who stood behind the Greenies table wearing a "Save the Tigers" T-shirt. "I have to say, I think we have the most creative booth here." She waved a hand at their long table, covered with petitions to sign, baked items (green-frosted cupcakes and cookies) for sale, and posters, including Maria's, that described ways people could help save the planet.

"And look at this cutie," Ms. Sharma added, reaching out to pet Angel. "She's sure to attract some attention, too. You gave the Greenies a great plug on the news!" She held up a hand for a high five, and Lizzie slapped it.

The Greenies booth did seem to be the most popular one at the fair. So many people stopped by to ask about adopting Angel that Lizzie finally put out a clipboard for everyone to write down their names and e-mail addresses on.

"Look at all these names," Lizzie told Maria later that afternoon. The fair was almost over but people were still coming by to meet and pet Angel. She loved the attention. She kissed everyone who petted her, and sat in every lap she could. "This list could come in handy next time we're looking for a home for a foster puppy."

"Right, because this one is already spoken for," said someone behind Lizzie.

Lizzie spun around to see Rose standing there, grinning at her. "Love the hair," Rose said. Then she knelt down and opened her arms to Angel. "Ready to go see your new home?" she asked, sweeping the puppy up.

Lizzie's heart sank. Rose really was going to take Angel. "But . . . you know, all Angel wants to do is be around people. She loves to sit in someone's lap, then maybe clown around a little and make them laugh."

"Great," Rose said. "Does she bark?"

Lizzie shook her head. "Well, no. And she doesn't shed much, either. She's a perfect apartment dog." Was Rose listening? Did she hear the hints Lizzie was giving?

"She's perfect in every way," said Rose. "At least, I think so. Can I take her for an overnight to make sure?" She was still holding Angel, and she did not look as if she was about to let go.

Lizzie was speechless. Finally, she answered. "I — I know you have first dibs," she told Rose, "and you deserve that. But I can't help it. I have to say it. I just don't think you're the right owner for Angel."

CHAPTER TEN

Rose stared at Lizzie. "Of course I'm not!" she said. "I'm way too busy right now to take on a dog, cute as this one may be."

"But . . ." Lizzie didn't understand.

"Didn't you get my voice mails?" Rose asked. "I was trying to tell you that I want my mother to adopt Angel." She shook her head. "It was really too complicated to explain on a phone message, and I kept getting cut off by the beep. That's why I wanted to come talk in person, but I've been so busy."

Lizzie shook her head. "You want Angel to live with your mom?" she asked.

Rose nodded. "I think it would be a perfect match," she said. "My mom was a scientist, studying ocean life. Now she's retired. She's still very independent and lives in her own apartment. But lately she had a fall, and since then she's had to use a walker. You know, one of those metal things that help people keep their balance?"

Lizzie nodded. She still didn't get where this was going.

"Anyway, my mom is too embarrassed to go out with her walker. 'I'm not some little old lady,' she always says, even though she kind of is." Rose rolled her eyes. "She doesn't like being seen hobbling around, so she stays home alone all day. I think she's lonely. She could use some company, especially company as adorable as this." She snuggled her nose into Angel's soft fur. "Plus, having a dog would force her to get outside. Dogs can't be indoors all day long. Right, Angel?"

She beamed down at Angel, and Angel gazed back up at her and wagged her tail.

That's right! We need fresh air just like everyone else.

Lizzie knew that Angel could be very happy with a lap to sit in, a person to entertain, and a few nice walks a day. She smiled at Rose. "Sounds good to me."

"So Angel spent the night with Rose's mother?" Maria asked the next morning as she and Lizzie walked up the main entrance steps to school together.

Lizzie nodded. "I miss her so much already, but I'm still hoping that Rose's mom likes her. I haven't heard anything yet. Mom says no news is good news, but I'm still keeping my fingers crossed."

"How did your mom like your hair?" Maria asked as she pulled open one of the big doors.

Lizzie shrugged. "She was pretty surprised, but then she was actually okay with it. She said she's been thinking about trying a few purple high-lights herself."

Inside, the hall was full of kids. Lizzie had been expecting to get a lot of attention and stares because of her green hair — but instead she was the one who was staring. A lot of kids in the hall had green hair just like hers!

"Go, Greenies!" yelled a boy named Noah, who had curly green hair.

"Greenies rule!" said another boy with a green buzz cut.

"Yay, Greenies!" A girl with long green hair waved at Lizzie.

Maria smiled at Lizzie's stunned expression. "The hair chalk sold out. Didn't you notice?"

Lizzie shook her head. "I guess I was too busy with Angel and all her admirers," she said. She looked around at all the green heads in the hall. "Yikes," she said. "I hope I'm not going to get in trouble with Ms. Guzman." Lizzie had never been sent to the principal's office, but Charles had, and he'd reported that she could be pretty strict.

"I kind of doubt that," said Maria with a funny smile. She pointed over Lizzie's shoulder.

Lizzie turned to see Ms. Guzman striding toward her, a big pouf of green replacing her normally straight gray hair. "Love it, Lizzie," she said. "Maybe we should have Green Hair Day every spring."

Lizzie was like a celebrity all day at school. Not only had she been on TV, but she was the girl who had started the green-hair trend. People pointed and whispered when she went by, and other kids gave her fist bumps or high fives when they passed her in the hall.

The best part was the Greenies meeting that day after school. The room was full. And the new attendees weren't only kids! There were more high schoolers and adults in the room, too. The Greenies club was growing fast.

"Great work, Lizzie," said Ms. Sharma, who was standing near the door when Lizzie walked in. "We doubled our membership in one day. Think of all the great things we can get done now!"

Lizzie just had to laugh. Ms. Sharma's hair was green, too!

"Is there room for two — or should I say three — more?" asked someone behind Lizzie.

She turned to see Rose standing in the doorway with an older woman next to her. The woman leaned on a metal walker. Her cheeks were pink and she was smiling. Angel stood by her side, wagging her tail and wearing a sweet doggy grin.

"This is my mom," said Rose, "Carolyn Fontana."

"Not Dr. Carolyn Fontana," said Ms. Sharma. "The shark expert?"

The older woman smiled and nodded. "Call me Caro," she said.

Ms. Sharma introduced herself and Lizzie. "Lizzie, Dr. Fontana was responsible for some truly groundbreaking research on great white sharks. She is an amazing woman, an inspiration to every scientist."

Lizzie nodded and smiled. "Cool," she said. That was great, but at the moment, she wasn't really interested in sharks. There was only one question on her mind. "Are you going to adopt Angel?" she asked as she bent to scoop the little dog into her arms.

"Absolutely," said Rose's mom. "We fell in love at first sight, didn't we, girl?" She smiled at Angel. "We've been on three walks already today, and then I just decided to come to this meeting

Rose told me about. She knows how much I care about the environment, and she said maybe you'd let me join."

Rose smiled at Lizzie and nodded. Angel had been just the right medicine for her mother.

"The Greenies would be thrilled and honored to have you as a member," said Ms. Sharma. "Maybe you'll tell us a bit about your research someday."

Lizzie let Angel down and ran to get a chair for Rose's mom. The minute the older woman sat down, Angel leapt into her lap and stretched up to lick her cheek.

This is where I belong.

Lizzie could see that Dr. Fontana and Angel were meant for each other. "Welcome to the Greenies," she said. "Welcome to both of you."

PUPPY TIPS

Angel is not an official therapy dog, but she sure is good medicine for Dr. Fontana, cheering her up and getting her out of the house. In a sense, all dogs are therapy dogs: pets help us live happier, healthier lives in so many ways.

• Kids who are exposed to dogs and cats early in their lives may develop fewer allergies as they age.

• Pet owners are known to have better heart health: lower cholesterol and blood pressure. This is probably because being around animals reduces stress in general.

• Dogs get us out of the house to exercise and help us socialize with other people while we're out there. Taking a walk with your dog is a huge boost for your physical and mental health.

I know it works for me. In fact, I'm about to head out for a walk with Zipper, right now!

Dear Reader,

I'm often asked where I get my ideas. In this case, I read about it in the news. I have seen several newspaper and Internet stories over the years about dogs that were trapped on cliffs. Doesn't that sound like an exciting way to start a story? I had a great time imagining and then writing about the details of Angel's rescue. I hope reading this story was as much fun for you as writing it was for me.

Yours from the Puppy Place,

Ellen Miles

THE PUPPY PLACE

DON'T MISS THE NEXT PUPPY PLACE ADVENTURE!

Here's a sneak peek at JAKE!

"I don't know," said Lizzie. "I guess I'm still not getting it, but how can it be any fun when all you do is work?"

"Trust me," said Maria. "It's so much fun. More fun than Disneyland. More fun than Halloween."

Lizzie raised an eyebrow. Sometimes Maria exaggerated. Could horse camp really be better than Halloween?

Lizzie Peterson and her best friend, Maria Santiago, were on their way to Appletree Farm, a horse camp in the country. Maria had been to Appletree twice before, once for an introductory weekend and once for a whole ten-day session in the summer. Maria was horse-crazy and had been riding since she was three or something.

Lizzie, on the other hand, was not quite so horse-crazy. Until recently, in fact, she had pretty much been afraid of horses. They were big, they were unpredictable, and their hooves and teeth were huge. Who wouldn't be afraid? Now that she had taken a bunch of lessons at the stable where Maria usually rode, Lizzie felt a lot less nervous around horses, but she still liked dogs better.

Lizzie was even crazier about dogs than Maria was about horses. Her goal in life was to spend as much time as possible around dogs. Helping out at her aunt Amanda's doggy day care; volunteering at Caring Paws, the local animal shelter; and helping run a dog-walking business (Maria was one of her partners) would have been plenty for most people. Not for Lizzie. She had also convinced her parents that their family (her dad, a firefighter; her mom, a newspaper reporter; and her two younger brothers, Charles and the Bean) should become a foster family for puppies. They had tried it, and everybody liked it (even Mom, who was really more of a cat person), so they kept on doing it.

By now everybody in Littleton knew that the Petersons were the people to turn to if you heard about a puppy in need of help. The Petersons had taken care of dozens of puppies, keeping each one until they had found it the perfect forever home. Lizzie loved getting to know the puppies and figuring out what kind of home would be best for each one, depending on its personality. She knew how important it was to make a good match: people who hated exercise should not adopt a dog who loved and needed a lot of it, for example.

The best match ever was the one they'd made for Buddy, a sweet brown-and-white mixed-breed puppy the Petersons had fostered — then ended up adopting. Buddy was a part of the family now, and Lizzie loved him more than anything in the world.

"Buddy face," said Maria now, as they drove along a bumpy country road. "You're thinking about him, aren't you?" She could always tell when Lizzie was thinking about her puppy. "You've got that certain smile."

Maria's father glanced in the rearview mirror and grinned at Lizzie. "Even I can tell when you're thinking about Buddy," he said. "You sure do love that puppy, don't you?"

ABOUT THE AUTHOR

Ellen Miles loves dogs, which is why she has a great time writing the Puppy Place books. And guess what? She loves cats, too! (In fact, her very first pet was a beautiful tortoiseshell cat named Jenny.) That's why she came up with the Kitty Corner series. Ellen lives in Vermont and loves to be outdoors with her dog, Zipper, every day, walking, biking, skiing, or swimming, depending on the season. She also loves to read, cook, explore her beautiful state, play with dogs, and hang out with friends and family.

Visit Ellen at www.ellenmiles.net.